THE BUTTERCUP FARM FAMILY

"Well, I know what *I* should like to do," said Ann. "I know where *I'd* like to go."

"Where?" asked Mummy.

"To Buttercup Farm, of course — Uncle Ned's farm," said Ann. "It's a lovely place."

"Oh, *yes* — we went there a year ago," said Mike. "I like Uncle Ned and Auntie Clara. Oh, Daddy, if we went for six months we could really help properly on the farm. There'd be all kinds of things to do."

"That really is a splendid idea," said Mummy.

30 p

The Buttercup Farm Family

Enid Blyton

*Illustrated by Joyce Smith
and David Dowland*

Beaver Books

A Beaver Book
Published by Arrow Books Limited
62-65 Chandos Place, London WC2N 4NW

An imprint of Century Hutchinson Limited

London Melbourne Sydney Auckland
Johannesburg and agencies throughout
the world

First published in 1951 by Lutterworth Press
Sparrow edition 1981
Reprinted 1984
Beaver edition 1989

Made and printed in Great Britain by
Courier International Ltd, Tiptree, Essex

ISBN 0 09 926050 6

CONTENTS

AN EXCITING PLAN

EVERYONE at school called Mike, Belinda and Ann the Caravan Family, because they lived in two caravans. They thought it would be lovely to do that.

"I wish *I* went home to a caravan every Friday like you do," said Susan to Ann.

"It must be such fun," said Tom to Mike. "I suppose when you get tired of being in one place, you just put in your horses and wander away!"

"Do ask me to spend a week-end with you!" said Hilda to Belinda. "I've never even been inside a caravan. I do so want to see what it's like."

Mike, Belinda and Ann loved the two caravans they lived in with their mother and father at the week-ends. They were yellow, painted here and there with red. Davey and Clopper were the two horses that pulled the caravans along, when the family wanted to move somewhere else.

"Once we went to Granny's in our caravans," said Ann, remembering. "She let us have them in her back garden. I liked that."

It was at the end of the Christmas holidays now. The Caravan Family had been to Granny's for Christmas Day and Boxing Day. After that the snow came, and Mummy said that living in caravans wasn't so much fun then. The children loved the snow, and had built a most enormous snowman outside their own caravan, which quite scared the two horses when they first caught sight of it.

One afternoon the children went to their parents' caravan and saw Daddy and Mummy sitting there, talking excitedly to one another.

"But what about the children?" Mummy was saying. "We can't possibly take them with us. What shall we do with them?"

"Granny will have them," said Daddy.

Belinda burst into the caravan at once.

"Mummy, Daddy! What are you talking about? Where are you going without us? Oh, please, please don't go!"

"Oh, dear—did you hear what we were

A most enormous snowman

saying?" said Mummy. "I didn't want to tell you till everything was decided."

"What? Tell us what it is," said Mike. "I don't want you to go away and leave us."

"Well, we'll tell you," said Daddy. "Come in and sit down, all three of you— and don't look so upset, it's nothing dreadful!"

Mike, Belinda and Ann came in, shut the door, and sat down in the caravan. Daddy waved a letter at them.

"I've just had a most exciting letter. It's

an invitation to Mummy and me to go to America for six months, from my brother out there—your Uncle Harry. A holiday like that would be so lovely for Mummy."

"But—but—would you leave us behind?" said Ann, looking very unhappy.

"Yes, we should have to," said Daddy. "But you are all big enough to look after yourselves now, and if anything happened Mummy and I could fly back and be with you in a day. So you needn't worry about anything."

"Would you like to go very much, Mummy?" asked Mike.

Mummy nodded. "Yes. Daddy and I haven't had a proper holiday alone together for years and years. I don't want to leave the three of you—but I'm sure you'd be all right with Granny."

"Well, then," said Mike, suddenly putting on a very brave look, "you go, Mummy. We won't be selfish and make a fuss. You deserve a holiday. Doesn't she, Daddy?"

"She certainly does," said Daddy, and he put his arm round Mummy and kissed her. "Thanks, Mike, for being so nice about it."

"I'll be nice too," said Ann, though she looked as if she was going to burst into tears at any moment.

Belinda hugged her mother.

"I'll look after the others," she said. "You needn't worry a bit about them, Mummy."

"Thank you, darling," said Mummy. "Now we'll go and ring up Granny and see if she can have you."

But oh dear, Granny couldn't have them after all! Daddy came back from telephoning looking quite upset.

"Granny can't have the children," he said. "She has asked her two little great-nephews to stay this year, because their mother is very ill and can't look after them for months."

"Well, I know what *I* should like to do," said Ann. "I know where *I'd* like to go."

"Where?" asked Mummy.

"To Buttercup Farm, of course—Uncle Ned's farm," said Ann. "Fancy you not thinking of it, Mummy! It's a lovely place."

"Oh, *yes*—we went there a year ago,"

said Mike. "I like Uncle Ned and Auntie Clara. Oh, Daddy, if we went for six months we could really help properly on the farm. There'd be all kinds of things to do."

"That really is a splendid idea," said Mummy.

By the next day everything was arranged. Uncle Ned said he and Auntie Clara would love to have the children for six whole months and they were to come right away!

"We'll set off on Thursday," said Daddy. "Maybe the snow will have cleared by then, and Davey and Clopper will get a foothold on the roads. Ned will be glad to have both horses to help on the farm, I'm sure. The caravans can stand in a barn somewhere at the farm till we come back again."

So on Thursday the little family set off to Uncle Ned's. The children were all excited. To live on a farm for six months—what could be better than that, with the spring-time just coming on?

"We're going to Buttercup Farm!" sang Ann, as they went jogging along in the caravans. "Buttercup Farm, Buttercup Farm! We're going to Buttercup Farm!"

O N the way to Buttercup Farm
Clopper slipped on the frosty road
and fell down with a crash. Ann
screamed in fright.

"Clopper! You've hurt yourself!"

Daddy leapt down and ran to poor old
Clopper. Clopper looked up at him out of
puzzled brown eyes that seemed to say,
"What has happened? I'm frightened."

"Get up, then, old fellow," said Daddy,
gently. "Let's see if you're hurt. No—
you haven't broken your leg, old boy.
You're all right."

But Clopper simply wouldn't get up. He
lay there on the road, and wouldn't move.
Daddy and Mike tugged at him, but he was
much too heavy.

He lay there for almost three hours, and
Daddy was quite in despair. "We'll have
to go to the nearest farm and get ropes and

a couple of men and pull him up," he said. "He really must have hurt himself somewhere, poor old boy."

Daddy got two men and a strong rope—and then, as they hurried over to Clopper, a surprising thing happened. Clopper heaved himself over, gave a funny groan, and stood up! He seemed a bit wobbly, but certainly he had no broken legs.

"Look at that, now!" said one of the men. "Just thought he'd lie down for a rest! Nothing wrong with *him*. Bit scared, I expect, after slipping like that. You walk at his head, sir, for a while."

So Daddy walked at Clopper's head, and he seemed to be quite all right. But how late it made them all in arriving at Buttercup Farm!

"Instead of arriving at half-past two, we shan't be there till half-past five, in the dark," said Mummy. "And we shall all be so cold and hungry. Oh dear, whatever will Auntie Clara say when we arrive so late!"

It was quite dark when the two caravans reached Buttercup Farm. There was the

A dog came bounding to meet them

farmhouse, with lights shining out of all the downstairs windows. A dog came bounding to meet them, barking loudly.

"Oh, Gilly!" cried Ann, pleased. "You know us, don't you, and you're so pleased to see us."

Gilly was a spaniel, with lovely long, drooping ears and a silky coat. She licked each of the children in turn and then ran barking indoors to tell Auntie Clara that the family had arrived.

Auntie Clara gave them a lovely welcome. She stood at the door, plump and beaming, and a most delicious smell came from the house. The hungry children sniffed it eagerly.

"Oooh—bacon and eggs, isn't it? Just what I feel like!" said Mike. "Hullo, Auntie Clara! We're late because Clopper fell down on the frosty roads, and wouldn't get up."

"Oh, you poor things—you must be so cold and hungry," said kind Auntie Clara, and she took their cold hands in her warm ones, and pulled them into the house.

"Ned, Ned!" she called to her husband.

"See to the horses for them—they're all so tired and hungry!"

"I'm going to love living with you, Auntie Clara," said Ann, pleased to be in the warm farmhouse kitchen with its big red fire.

"That's right," said Auntie Clara. "Now, if you're not too tired, there's hot water in the bathroom, and then there's a hot meal down here, just waiting to be served. So hurry!"

They hurried. They were soon downstairs again, sitting round the big wooden table. Ann liked it because it was quite round. "Nobody can sit at the top or the bottom, because it's round," she said to Belinda.

Bacon and eggs. New bread and honey. Hot scones with creamy farm butter. A great big fruit cake with almonds on top. Big mugs of creamy milk. What a meal! Mummy looked round at the hungry children and smiled.

"Clara, if you feed them like this all the time, I shan't know them when I come back. They'll be so big and fat!"

"Like Uncle Ned," said Belinda, and

they all laughed. Uncle Ned was very big indeed, and getting rather fat, but all the children loved him because he was so jolly.

"Where are Davey and Clopper?" said Ann. "Are they having a meal too?"

"Of course," said Uncle Ned. "Let me see, Clara, did we send bacon and eggs out to them—or was it scones and butter?"

"Uncle Ned, you always make jokes," said Ann. "Nobody would give horses bacon and eggs."

"Well, you're a clever little girl, so I dare say you're right," said Uncle Ned with one of his booming laughs. "You needn't worry your head about Davey and Clopper, little Ann. They're in the stables along with my horses, eating a fine meal of oats. And the caravans are put into the big barn, where they're saying how-do-you-do to the wagons and the carts!"

"It's lovely to be at Buttercup Farm," said Belinda. "Oh, Auntie Clara, you really *will* let us help, won' you? I want to feed the hens."

"And I'm going to milk the cows," said Mike.

"And I shall look after the piglets if you've got any," said Ann.

"You shall all help," said Auntie Clara. "But mind, now—farming is hard work, and you'll have to stick to your jobs and do them well, week in and week out! Just like real farmers do."

"Oh, we will," said Mike earnestly. "It's very kind of you to have us, and we'll be sure to do all we can."

"Now—if you've all finished, I think it's time Ann went to bed," said Mummy. "And then, Belinda, you come along with Mike."

"So *early*!" said Mike, surprised.

"Ah," said Uncle Ned, "early to bed and early to rise is the farmer's motto, young man. There are no lie-abeds here! Breakfast at seven o'clock sharp!"

"I don't care if it's at six!" said Mike. "So long as I'm at Buttercup Farm!"

IT was lovely to wake up in the morning at Buttercup Farm. It was still dark, but all sorts of noises were going on outside the windows.

"Clank, clank! Clipper-clop! Hrrrumph! Mooooooo-ooo! Quack, quack!"

It was a quarter to seven. Mike got up and went to the window, but it was still too dark to see anything. He put his head into the girls' room.

"Oh, you're getting up! I'm just going to," said Mike. "Doesn't everything wake up early on a farm—even before it's light!"

"Yes. I heard the cows mooing," said Ann, dragging on her jersey. "I suppose they're being milked. And I heard Clopper *hrrrumph* like he always does when he wants to get out of the stable."

They all had breakfast in the great big

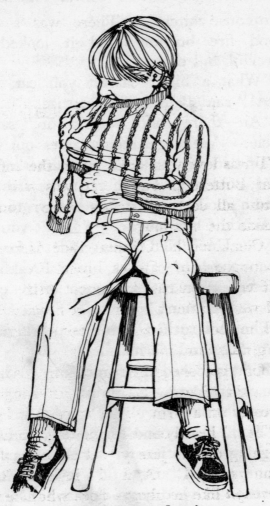

Ann dragging on her jersey

farmhouse kitchen. There was a bright wood fire burning, and it looked very cheerful and cosy.

"What a big breakfast you eat, Uncle Ned!" said Belinda, in surprise.

"Ah—there's hard work to do," said her uncle. "We're getting potatoes out of the clamps to-day, to send to market. That's hard, cold work out there in the frost. We need a good breakfast to get down to that!"

Auntie Clara laughed. "Don't you listen to your Uncle Ned making excuses for eating so much! He eats as big a breakfast on Sunday, when he leaves most of the outside jobs to the men!"

They all tucked into the porridge, cold ham, toast and marmalade.

Belinda looked at her mother. "When are you going away, Mummy?" she asked. "Not yet, are you?"

"Well, Daddy and I have to go to London to get some clothes for our American trip," Mummy said, "and to do a few other things. We thought we'd go to-day, and then stay in London till it's time to leave by plane."

"Oh, I *wish* I could fly over with you!"

said Mike at once. "That would be almost better than living on a farm."

"What about school?" asked Belinda, suddenly thinking of all kinds of things. "And what about . . ."

"You needn't worry about anything, darling," said Mummy. "It's all arranged. You are so near to your school here that you can go there by bus each day, which is very lucky. You can sleep at Buttercup Farm each night."

"That sounds lovely," said Ann. "I don't want to miss school, but I don't want to miss a minute of Buttercup Farm either. Mummy, won't it be lovely?—we shall be here long enough to see exactly what goes on at the farm right up to summer-time."

"Lovely!" said Mummy. "You must write and tell us all about everything each week, and we'll write and tell you about New York and the buildings that are called skyscrapers because they almost touch the clouds."

"I'd like to climb up to the top of one and catch a cloud," said Ann. "I'd tie it to my wrist and fly it like a balloon."

"Isn't she a baby!" said Mike, and everyone laughed.

After breakfast the children went in the car to the station with Mummy and Daddy. They said good-bye quite happily, because they knew their parents were going to have a lovely holiday, and they knew that they themselves were going to have a splendid time at Buttercup Farm.

"Now mind you're good and helpful," said Mummy. "And be kind to everyone, and remember to say your prayers every single night, and be sure to put Daddy and me into them."

"Well, of *course*," said Belinda, "Oh, here comes the train. And now, oh dear, I don't want to say good-bye!"

"Don't say it then," said Daddy sensibly, and that made Belinda laugh. She yelled good-bye with the others, and waved madly. The train went out of the station and the children turned to go back to the farm.

"I vote we go all over the farm, and see what animals there are, and find out where everything is," said Mike.

The others thought that was a very good

" I didn't like to go too near."

idea, so they spent the day having a "good old wander", as Auntie Clara called it. They were very tired and rather dirty by the time tea-time came—but, dear me, they knew a great deal more about the farm!

"We saw Jamie and Jinny the sheep-dogs," said Mike, "and all the sheep on the hills."

"And we saw all your hens. You've got thirty-three, Auntie," said Ann. "I counted them when they went in to roost."

"Well, fancy that!" said Auntie Clara. "I never knew how many hens I had before!"

"And fifteen ducks," went on Ann, "and

" You've got about nine cats."

six geese. I don't know how many turkeys, because they gobbled at me and I didn't like to go too near."

"There are seventeen," said Mike. "And we saw all the cows, Uncle Ned, and we know all their names—Clover, Buttercup, Daisy, Sorrel, Blackie, Whitey . . ."

"Thank you—I know them too!" said Uncle Ned. "Did you see the horses? Fine creatures they are."

"Oh, *yes*—lovely!" said Mike. "I like the ones with shaggy heels, Uncle. They're so enormous, and I like their big manes and shining coats. They're proper farm-horses, aren't they?"

"Yes—strong as giants," said Uncle Ned. "Best workers I've got."

"And we saw the old sow," said Ann. "She's enormous too. And did you know you've got about nine cats, Uncle?"

"I hope we have!" said Uncle Ned, with his booming laugh. "We've got about a thousand mice and as many rats—so nine cats are none too many, little Ann! Well, well, you've certainly been round the farm to-day. Did you like it?"

"We *loved* it!" said all three at once. "It's the nicest farm in the world!"

IT was such fun spending the days at Buttercup Farm, even though it was winter-time. There was always something to do. The hens to feed, the cows to bring in, the hay to be fetched, and the firewood to be brought to the kitchen door for Auntie Clara.

One day Ann went to see the old shepherd, who lived in a little hut up on the hills with his sheep. He was a bent old man, with a wrinkled, smiling face, and eyes that twinkled merrily. His name was Willie.

Willie beckoned to Ann to come close to him. Near his hut he had built a little sheep-pen, fenced in with stakes. It was spread with straw.

"Lookee here, Missy," he said. "See what I've got to-day. They came in the night."

Ann looked. She saw a big mother sheep,

"*Lookee here, Missy.*"

and beside her two tiny lambs—so small that they almost looked like big toy ones.

"Oh! Are they real?" said Ann. "Do, *do* let me go in and stroke them."

"No—the old mother wouldn't like it," said the shepherd. "They're the first lambs of the season on Buttercup Farm. We'll soon be having plenty more. You must come and see me every day, little Missy, then I can show you all the new-born lambs I've got."

"Oh, I will," said Ann, earnestly. "I'd like that better than anything. Can I play with them when they get bigger, Willie?"

"Oh, yes—they'll love to have you skipping about with them," said the old shepherd, and his eyes twinkled at Ann.

"Willie—I suppose you couldn't *possibly* give me a lamb for my own, like the one Mary had in the rhyme that goes 'Mary had a little lamb' could you?" said Ann, her eyes shining at the thought.

The shepherd shook his head. "Oh no, Missy, I couldn't take a lamb away from its ma. It would fret. Look, here are Jamie and Jinny come to talk to you. They're my dogs, you know—hard-working sheep-dogs."

"Do they work for you, then?" asked Ann, surprised. "What do they do?"

"They be wonderful dogs," said Willie, and he stroked Jinny gently. "My old legs are getting tired and bent now, and I can't go chasing the sheep uphill and downhill like I used to. So Jamie and Jinny do all that for me. When I want to move the sheep to another hill, these dogs take them for me. I'll show you them at work one day."

"How clever they must be," said Ann. "I must go now, Willie. I'll come to-morrow and see if you've got any more new lambs to show me."

She ran off to tell Mike and Belinda what she had seen.

Every day after that the little girl went trudging up to the hill to see old Willie and to look at the new-born lambs.

One day he showed her a weakly little lamb.

"Poor mite!" he said. "Looks as if it will die. Its mother won't feed it, and the other ewes won't have anything to do with it either."

"Poor little thing!" said Ann. "I wish I could feed it, Willie. Wouldn't it drink out of a spoon, if I gave it milk like that?"

"No, Missy. But it would drink out of a baby's bottle," said Willie. "You ask your aunt if she'll let you have this lamb down at the farm-house to feed. She'll give you an old bottle and a teat for the lamb to suck through."

Ann stared at Willie as if she couldn't believe her ears. "*Willie!* Oh, Willie—are you *giving* me this lamb? For my own—to feed and look after?"

"Well—it sounds like it!" said the old shepherd, laughing. "See you don't get tired of the little mite, now. You'll have to feed it many times a day, with any milk your aunt has to spare."

Ann held out shaking arms as the shepherd put the tiny lamb into them, and then, almost crying with joy, she went carefully down the hill.

"Mike!" she called. "Belinda! Look what I've got—for my very own. A lamb! A real

"For my very own" live lamb whose mother doesn't want it."

Mike and Belinda stared in amazement. Ann took the lamb into the kitchen.

"Auntie Clara! Dear Auntie Clara, look what Willie's given me—a poor lamb without a kind mother. He says I can keep it and feed it if you'll let me. Will you?"

"Well, well, well!" said Auntie Clara, and she fetched a bottle from the cupboard, and put a rubber teat on it. "Poor wee thing! Yes, of course you can feed it, child, and care for it. Many's the little lamb I've fed and brought up myself! Belinda, get the warm milk off that stove. I'll give it to the lamb."

"Let *me*, let *me*," said Ann. "It's my lamb. *I* want to feed it, Auntie."

Auntie Clara let her, of course. The tiny lamb smelt the milk as Auntie Clara squeezed a little out of the teat, and nuzzled at it. In a moment he was sucking away at it, drinking the warm milk as fast as he could! He stood up on his tiny legs, looking just like a big toy lamb.

"He's beautiful! Look at him!" said Ann in joy. "Auntie, he's swelling up fat already with the milk. He'll soon be well and strong, won't he? Oh, Auntie, fancy, I've got a lamb of my very very own!"

"What will you call him?" asked Mike. "I should call him Wobbly. Look how wobbly he is on his legs!"

"What a horrid name!" said Ann. "No— I shall call him Hoppetty, because soon he'll be hopping and skipping all over the place!"

"You love him so much that I expect you'll put him into your prayers," said Belinda. "You always put Davey and Clopper in, don't you, our two horses?"

"Yes. And now Hoppetty too," said Ann. "Oh, I'm so happy. I never, never thought in all my life I'd have a lamb of my very own."

THE three children were very sorry when the holidays came to an end, and they had to go to school. But after a day or two at school they decided it was great fun to be back again with all their friends.

"And it's lovely to go home at the end of the day to Buttercup Farm," said Belinda. "I keep wondering how many eggs the hens have laid, and if there are any piglets yet."

"And I keep thinking of Hoppetty," said Ann, "and hoping he hasn't got into mischief, and wondering if Auntie Clara's given him his milk."

"Well, you needn't wonder *that*," said Mike. "You know she'd never never forget. Anyway, Hoppetty's so cheeky now that he'd be sure to go and remind her if she did forget. He'd go and put his front hooves up on her skirt, like he does to you."

"Yes. He's *sweet* when he does that," said Ann.

The weeks went by and February came in with snowdrops and hazel catkins blowing in the wind.

"They shake and wriggle on the hedges just like Hoppetty wriggles his tail when he drinks his milk," said Ann. "I suppose that's why the catkins are called lambs' tails!"

Belinda had got very interested in the hens. She wanted to look after them for Auntie Clara, who, now that she suddenly had three children to see to, found that her hands were very full indeed. So she was glad to let Belinda help.

"Now," she said, "I want to know first if you mean to help properly, every week, and every day of the week—or if you only want to try looking after the hens for a few days, just for fun. You must tell me honestly, and then stick to what you say."

"Auntie, I want to help properly," said Belinda. "I won't get tired of it and give up. I promise I won't. Well—if I *do* get tired, I still won't give up! Will that do?"

Hazel catkins blowing in the wind

"Yes. I'll trust you," said Auntie Clara. "You see, Belinda, when we have animals or birds in our care, we have to be very, very trustable, because if we are not, they go hungry or thirsty, or may be cold and unhappy."

"I wouldn't let that happen," said Belinda. "I really am trustable, Auntie."

"Yes, I think you are," said Auntie Clara. "You have certainly never forgotten anything I asked you to do, and, what is more, you have done all your jobs well. Very well, then—you may have the hens to look after!"

"Oh, *thank you!*" said Belinda. "I think I know all I have to do, Auntie—feed them with hot mash in the morning—feed them again when I come home from school—always give them fresh water—see that they have straw in their nesting-boxes—put fresh peat on the hen-house floor when it needs it. That's all, isn't it?"

"What about cleaning the house out three times a week?" said Mike, who was listening. "You don't like *that* job, Belinda. You say you hate the smell in the hen-house when it wants cleaning. I bet you won't do that!"

"No, she won't," said Uncle Ned, joining in suddenly. "You'll do that, Mike! It's a boy's job, that."

Mike went red and wished he had offered to clean the hen-house himself, before Uncle said anything about it. But Belinda had other ideas.

"Oh, *no*! I'm going to do everything, thank you!" she said. "Cleaning the house out too. I know I don't like it much, but I'm not going to be the sort of person who just chooses the bit she likes and leaves the nasty part to other people."

"Well, there now!" said Auntie Clara admiringly. "That's the way to talk, isn't it, Ned? We can easily find Mike some other job. I'm sure Belinda will do the cleaning just as well as Mike or anyone."

Belinda took the hens very seriously indeed. She even wanted to lift the heavy pail of cooked food down from the kitchen stove each morning, to take to the hens, but Auntie Clara wouldn't let her do that. "No. It's too heavy. You just think what's in it—

all the bits and pieces and scraps, all the old potatoes we don't want, all the peel, everything that's over from the food prepared for this big household! I'll lift it down for you. You can stir in the mash to make it nice for the hens."

So Belinda stirred in big spoonfuls of mash, and she put a dose of cod-liver oil for

the hens each day too, because Auntie Clara said it was very good for them in the cold weather. Belinda never forgot.

She always saw that the hens had clean water, and if by chance it had frozen hard, she put in fresh water. She gave them plenty of fine soft peat in the hen-house, and stuffed their nest-boxes with straw.

The hens soon grew to know Belinda

The hens soon grew to know Belinda, and came running to her as soon as she appeared, clucking excitedly. Auntie Clara complained that they came walking into her kitchen to find Belinda when she had gone to school!

"I'll have to shut them up in their yard, and not let them run loose," she said, jokingly.

"Oh, *no*!" said Belinda at once. "They wouldn't like that, Auntie. They do so like to run loose and scratch over the ground everywhere. Please don't shut them up."

At night, when dusk came down on the farmyard, Belinda went out to her hens. She called to them in her clear little voice. "Chookies, chookies, chookies! Bedtime! Come along then! Out of the hedges and out of the field. Chookies, chookies, chookies!"

And obediently all the hens came rushing from every direction, and Belinda took them to their house. Up the slanting boards they ran, and settled on the perches to roost, cuddling close up to one another sleepily.

"Good chookies," said Belinda, shutting and locking the door. "Lay me plenty of eggs to-morrow!"

"Cluck, cluck," answered the hens, almost asleep.

And will you believe it, the very next day they laid twenty-seven eggs for Belinda to take proudly into the house. She had to take two baskets to carry them in. How pleased Auntie Clara was!

"Well! You're doing better with the hens than I ever did!" said her aunt. "I really do feel proud of you!"

ONE day, when Ann went to tell Willie the shepherd the latest tale about Hoppetty the lamb, who was growing fat and very mischievous, he told her something exciting.

"You won't be at school this afternoon, will you?" he said. "It's Saturday. Well, how would you like to come along and see Jamie and Jinny do some real good work for me?"

"What sort of work?" asked Ann, thrilled.

"Well, I want to move the sheep away from this hill," said Willie. "I want them to go over to that hill yonder, where there's some good grass for them. My old legs won't walk fast enough to do work like that now—so I'm going to get Jamie and Jinny to do it for me."

The two big sheep-dogs heard their names

and wagged their tails hard. They looked up adoringly at Willie, their long pink tongues hanging out.

All around were the sheep

"But Willie—can they really take the sheep all by themselves?" asked Ann, astonished. "And what about that bridge down there, over the stream—will they make the sheep cross that? I'm sure they won't want to."

"Ah, it won't matter if they want to or not," said Willie, with a smile. "They'll go, just the same. You be along at two o'clock, Missy, and bring your brother and sister too."

So, at two o'clock sharp, Mike, Belinda and Ann were up by the shepherd's hut. All around were the sheep, grazing peacefully. A few little lambs frisked about, kicking up their heels and making themselves a real nuisance to their mothers.

"Jamie! Jinny! Bunch them up!" said Willie suddenly to the two listening collies. In a trice they jumped up and ran to the sheep. "You watch them bunch them for me," said Willie, proudly. "They'll do it quicker than you could!"

And he was right. The two dogs ran round the sheep, barking loudly, and the startled animals ran together in alarm. They stood and looked at the dogs wonderingly.

One or two sheep didn't like being made to bunch together with the others. They trotted off, and some little lambs followed them in delight. Jamie went after them immediately. Wherever those sheep turned, there was Jamie, head down, barking, and at last in despair the runaway sheep and the naughty little lambs ran to join the big bunched-up flock.

"See? He's bunched them for me,"

said Willie. "Now they've got to take them down the hill and up the other side. Jamie! Jinny! Take them then! Down you go!"

The two clever dogs listened to Willie's orders, their tongues hanging out. They watched his arm as he waved it down the hill.

"They've understood you!" cried Mike. "Oh, Willie, aren't they marvellous? But I guess they won't find it easy to make the sheep cross that tiny bridge. Why, it's only a plank or two set across the stream!"

"Don't you worry!" said Willie. "The dogs will have them across in no time. Once they can get the first two or three sheep on the bridge they're all right. The rest will follow as sheep always do."

The three children watched eagerly. Down the hill in a big flock went the hurrying sheep—down, down, towards the water. They came to the bank and stopped. They didn't want to wade into the water, and they certainly couldn't jump across!

Jamie set to work to keep the sheep from scattering up and down the bank. Jinny wriggled through the crowd of sheep and got

behind one that stood near the little bridge.
The sheep suddenly found Jinny there and was
scared. It turned to the left. Jinny was there
too. It turned to the right. Jinny was at
once on the right. The sheep didn't know
what to do.

"Go over the bridge, silly, go over the
bridge!" shouted Ann, almost beside herself with excitement.

Jinny gave a sharp bark, and the sheep, in
the greatest alarm, trotted right across the
bridge to the other side. The sheep behind
at once followed it—and the next one and
the next.

The children laughed and laughed.

"It would be more difficult to stop them
now than to make them go across," said
Mike. "How silly sheep are! Look—
they're nearly all across. Oh—two or three
think they won't go."

But Jamie was behind the last few sheep,
and over they went, their little hooves
making a clip-clip-clip sound on the bridge.

"Now watch," said Willie. "The dogs
have bunched them, and taken them safely
across the water. They remember that

there are two good grazing grounds up there, one to the north and one to the south of the hill. They're looking at me to see which way I want them to go. Watch!"

Jamie and Jinny were both gazing hard at the old shepherd. He put his fingers to his mouth and gave a shrill whistle. Then he whistled again and waved his left arm. With one accord the dogs took the sheep to the south side of the hill, bunching them together first, and then running round and round them, forcing them the way they wanted them to go.

"See?" said Willie. "They know exactly what I want done, and they do it. I couldn't do without my dogs."

"They're wonderful!" said Ann. "Oh, Willie—I never *never* thought dogs could be so clever. I do love Jamie and Jinny. Don't you?"

"My best friends they are," said Willie gruffly. "You should see them go hunting for sheep lost in the snow, too. They won't come home till they've found them."

"There can't be any cleverer dogs in the world than Jamie and Jinny," said Mike.

"Oh, there are," said Willie. "You go to the sheep-dog trials, and see what other sheep-dogs can do with *strange* sheep. Wonderful good dogs they are."

Jamie and Jinny came running up. Willie took down a bag and shook out a heap of meaty bones for them.

"They deserve their wages," he said. And the three children thought so too!

THE children often talked about the two wonderful sheep-dogs, and marvelled at all they could do.

"There's only one lamb that won't take any notice of Jamie and Jinny," said Ann, proudly, "and that's Hoppetty. He just skips round them and says cheeky things in that funny little bleat of his."

"You're lucky, Ann," said Mike, who envied Ann her pet lamb. "So's Belinda. She's got heaps of hens that lay eggs for her, and you've got Hoppetty. I've got nothing of my own."

"Well, have a piglet when the old sow has her family," said Auntie Clara.

But Mike didn't want a piglet.

"I'd like a horse or a dog," he said. "Something that would follow me round like the hens follow Belinda, and like Hoppetty follows Ann. Auntie, did you know

" *I do love him so* "

that Hoppetty came all the way to the bus
the other day, when we went to school, and
Ann wanted to let him get on, but the
conductor wouldn't let him?"

Auntie Clara laughed. "I expect Ann
wanted Hoppetty to follow her to school,
like Mary in the nursery rhyme," she said.

"That's a bad little lamb you've got, Ann. He came into my dairy the other day and drank a whole pint of my cream!"

"Oh dear!" said Ann. "Don't make me put him in the field with the other sheep yet, Auntie. I do love him so."

Uncle Ned came in. "Heard the news?" he said.

"No, what?" cried the three children at once.

"Well—it's Willie's news really," said their uncle. "You'd better go and ask him what it is."

The children tore out of the house like wind. Up the hill they went to Willie. Jamie the sheep-dog came to meet them eagerly.

"Where's Jinny?" said Ann, missing the second dog. She was nowhere to be seen.

Willie came out of his hut when he saw the three children. He was smiling all over his brown, wrinkled old face. He beckoned to the children, and pointed inside his hut. They ran up to him.

"Got some news for you," he said, mysteriously. "You look in there."

They crowded into the little hut. Lying on some straw in the corner was Jinny. She looked very happy indeed. Ann gave a loud squeal of delight.

The children knelt down by Jinny

"Look! She's got some puppies! Oh, Willie, are they hers?"

"Hers and Jamie's," said Willie, proudly. "And a wonderful fine litter they be, Missy. Five of them, strong and healthy. Did ever you see such a sight?"

The children knelt down by Jinny, who didn't in the least mind their loud cries of admiration. She gave each pup a lick as if to say, "They're all mine! Don't you envy me?"

"The darlings!" said Belinda. "Oh, Willie, won't it be lovely to see them all grow up!"

Mike was looking at the tiny pups with shining eyes. He turned to Willie and put his hand earnestly on the old shepherd's arm. "Willie," he said, "please, please, Willie, could I have one of these pups for my own?"

Willie laughed. "Oh no, sonny. They are very valuable dogs, and they've all got new homes to go to. Soon as your uncle knew these pups were coming, he put the news around, and he's got orders for every one of them. When they're two months old they'll leave Jinny, and go to their new masters to learn their trade."

Mike was bitterly disappointed. "I never wanted anything so much in all my life," he said sadly, and Ann felt very sorry for him. So did Belinda. But if the pups were already sold, there was nothing more to be said.

They certainly were beautiful puppies.

They seemed to grow bigger each day, and when they at last had their eyes open they were really adorable.

"They roll about everywhere now, Auntie," Ann told her aunt some weeks later, "and one of them tries to walk, but he's very wobbly. Oh, I do wish they hadn't got to go away when they're so young—I wish we could see them grow up into fine big sheep-dogs."

"If I'd kept all the pups that the dogs here have had, I'd have about a hundred dogs running around," said Uncle Ned. "Jinny's pups are always good. They make wonderful dogs for the sheep on the hills round here, and there's many a dog you'll see at the sheep-dog trials that's been one of Jinny's youngsters."

When the pups grew old enough, they had to go to their new homes. The children had given all five of them names, and were very sad when the new masters came to fetch them.

Farmer Gray came for the pup called Tubby. Farmer Lawson came for Tinker, and a farmer's wife for Whiskers. Then a boy came for Scamp, and after that only little Rascal was left.

"He's the one I love most," said Mike, and he picked the puppy up and hugged him. The tiny thing licked his nose and gave a small whine.

"Uncle, who's having Rascal?" asked Ann at dinner-time that day. "Nobody has come for him yet."

"No, I know," said Uncle Ned. "The farmer who wanted him is leaving the district after all, and taking up fruit farming. He doesn't want a sheep-dog now. I don't know what to do with Rascal—can't seem to get anyone to buy him."

Mike was listening with all his ears. He went very red. "Uncle," he said, "I've got ten pounds saved up in the post office. *I'll* buy him. Please, please, do let me. I'll always love him and look after him well."

Uncle Ned and Auntie Clara looked at one another. Auntie Clara nodded. "Give him Rascal," she said. "He's been a good hard-working boy, Ned—cleaned out the dairy for me, fetched all my wood, done lots of jobs. He deserves a pup of his own."

"Right!" said Uncle Ned. "He's yours, Mike."

What a picture of joy Mike's face was. "A dog of my own," he said, in a funny low voice. "Oh, Uncle—it's the loveliest thing that's ever happened to me. A dog—of my very own!"

ONE morning Belinda came tearing
into the kitchen, where Ann and
Mike were doing their homework.
"Ann! Mike! The calves are born!
Oh, they're so sweet. Do, do come."

The homework was forgotten. Mike and
Ann raced after Belinda to the cow-sheds.
Calves! New calves for Buttercup Farm!
It really did sound very exciting.

After the children scampered Hoppetty,
Ann's lamb, and fat little Rascal, Mike's
pup. Jake the cowman was in the shed, and
he grinned as all the children came flying in.

"Now, now—what's the hurry? Anyone
would think you'd never seen calves before!"

"We've never seen such new ones," said
Belinda. "Oh, aren't they small—and what
long legs they've got! Sorrel, are you pleased
with them?"

Sorrel was the calves' mother, a big red and white cow with a very peaceful-looking face. She looked up at the children, and then bent her head down and licked one of her calves.

"She's got twins!" said Jake. "Your uncle's pleased about that. Two fine, strong calves they are, that anyone would be glad to have. Well, Sorrel, my beauty, you can be right proud of them!"

The twin calves soon grew to know the children, because they came a dozen times a day to see them. They marvelled at the way the tiny things could stand on their long legs, and it even seemed wonderful to Ann that they knew how to whisk their tails properly.

Auntie Clara said she would be very busy now, with two calves to feed and look after. "They will have to have milk to drink," she said, "but not milk with the cream on it—we can't spare that. They must have the separated milk, and I must put in cod-liver oil to make up for the cream."

"Like I give my hens," said Belinda at once. "Auntie, do the calves know how to *drink?* I thought new-born animals could only suck."

"Well, you come along to-morrow morning and watch me teach the calves to drink," said her aunt. "It's Saturday, so you'll be at home."

"We'll all come," said Ann. "I wouldn't miss a thing like that for anything!"

Next morning, all three children followed their aunt as she got ready the calves' meal. She filled two buckets with milk that had the cream taken from it, and shook some drops of cod-liver oil into the pails. Mike took one pail of milk for her and she took the other.

They went up to the cow-shed. Sorrel was out in the yard, with her calves near by. They were red and white, just like her. All three stared at Auntie Clara as she came along with the pail.

"The calves can suck, Auntie," said Ann. "I know that, because when I put my hand up, they take it into their mouth and suck my fingers hard!"

"Well, I shall use their sucking to help me to teach them to drink!" said Auntie Clara.

She set down her pail by one of the calves.
She dipped her hand into the pail and held
it out to the little calf.

He stared at Auntie Clara in surprise, but
didn't try to lick her hand, or even to suck
it. So Auntie Clara pushed her milky
fingers against the calf's soft nose. He smelt
the milk at once and sniffed at it. Then he
took Auntie Clara's fingers right into his
mouth and sucked hard, getting every drop
of milk.

"Oh, Auntie—what a long time it will
take to feed the calves like that," said
Belinda. "It'll take all day."

"No, no," said Auntie Clara. "Watch
me."

She dipped her hand into the pail again,
and held it out to the calf. He came nearer
to smell the milk on her fingers. In a trice
he was sucking at them again. Auntie Clara
drew her hand towards the pail. The calf
followed it, sucking hard. Auntie Clara
put her hand right down into the pail of
milk.

The calf's nose went down too, and in a
moment his mouth was right in the milk!

He went on sucking at Auntie Clara's hand, but because his mouth was in the milk he couldn't help *drinking* some too! He made a lot of noise about it and Ann laughed.

"Doesn't he sound rude? Oh, Auntie, that's very clever! You made him suck first, and then because he liked the sucking, his mouth followed your hand into the milk, and he found himself drinking too!"

"Yes," said Auntie Clara. "He'll soon be drinking well. And in a few days' time he'll be listening for the first clink of the pail, and will come tearing to meet me!"

"Can I teach the other twin?" begged Belinda. "Do, do let me! I know just how to."

"Very well," said Auntie Clara. "But don't let him upset the pail!"

Belinda dipped her hand in the milk and rubbed it gently against the other calf's mouth. He sniffed eagerly and began to suck her hand. She took it away and dipped it into the milk again. Once more the calf sucked her fingers, and this time she did just what Auntie Clara had done—lowered her hand gradually into the pail—and soon

Belinda helped to feed the calves

the hungry calf was half-sucking at her fingers and half-drinking out of the pail!

"I've done it!" said Belinda. "Oh, I do feel clever! Look at my calf, Auntie."

"It's been a most exciting morning," said Ann when the pails were empty. "There's always something lovely happening on a farm. I don't know why anybody bothers to live in a town when there are farms to live on."

Belinda helped her Aunt to feed the calves

every day—and before a week was up the twins raced to meet Belinda as soon as they heard the jingle of her pail-handle!

"You're lovely!" said Belinda. "I don't know who's the loveliest—you or—Hoppetty—or Rascal!"

"AUNTIE CLARA," said Belinda one day, when she came in from feeding the hens, "Auntie Clara, it's such a nuisance, there are two of my hens that won't stop sitting in the nesting-boxes. I keep shooing them out to run with the others, but back they go again as soon as my back is turned!"

Auntie Clara laughed. "Why, they're broody," she said.

"What's broody?" asked Ann.

"They want to sit on clutches of eggs and brood over them till they hatch," said her aunt. "Belinda, we'll get a clutch of thirteen eggs for each of them."

"Thirteen! What a funny number!" said Belinda.

"Not really," said her aunt. "It's just about as many as a hen can manage."

"I wish one of the *ducks* would go broody, and then we could put her on a clutch of duck eggs," said Mike. "I do love baby ducks."

"Well, if you like we'll put thirteen hen eggs under one broody hen and thirteen duck eggs under the other," said Auntie Clara. "Then you'll have plenty of young chicks and plenty of young ducklings too!"

"Oh—I *should* like that!" said Belinda at once. "It's the Easter holidays now, Auntie, so I shall have plenty of time to look after the hens. Where can I get the clutches of eggs?"

"Your uncle will get them," said Auntie Clara. "Mike, do you think you can go and look out two old coops to put the hens in? See if they want mending at all. They should be in the old barn."

Mike found them. One wanted a nail or two, but the other coop was all right. He carried them to Belinda. "Here you are," he said, "cages for your two broodies! Poor hens, they won't like being shut up in them."

"Oh, they won't mind," said Belinda. "You should see how they sit for hours and hours on the nesting-boxes! They will be very pleased to have nice coops like this to

Then she fetched a hen

sit in. I've asked Auntie what to do, and it's very easy."

Uncle Ned brought home two clutches of eggs. One clutch was made up of brown hen eggs. The other was of greeny-grey duck eggs, a little larger than the hen eggs.

Belinda arranged each clutch on some straw in a coop. Then she fetched a hen. She pushed her into the coop and shut her in. Then she went to fetch the other broody.

Mike and Ann watched the first hen. She stood in the coop and squawked. She looked at the clutch of eggs with her head on one side. She rearranged one or two with her beak, then she sat herself down very carefully on the whole thirteen and fluffed out her feathers so that she covered every single egg.

"She's sitting!" cried Ann to Belinda, as she came back with the other hen. "Look! She's happy."

Belinda put the second broody hen into the other coop. The hen stood for a minute or two as if puzzled and annoyed. She poked her head out between the bars of the coop, and then she sat herself down. A peaceful look came over her hen-face, and she fluffed herself out well.

"She likes the feel of all those eggs under her," said Belinda. "Auntie Clara, look! Both my broodies are sitting on eggs. Thirteen each. I shall have twenty-six new little birds!"

"Belinda's counting her chickens before they're hatched," said Mike with a grin. "Auntie, how long will it be before the eggs are hatched?"

"Three weeks for the hen eggs, and four for the duck eggs," said his aunt. "See that you look after the two hens well, Belinda."

"Of course, Auntie," said Belinda. And she did. She opened the coops every morning and lifted each squawking hen off the eggs. She gave them a good meal and let them run about for twenty minutes. Then back they had to go into the coops again.

"The eggs mustn't get cold," she told Ann. "If they do, they won't hatch. A hen mother is much better than a duck mother, because ducks often leave their eggs to get cold."

The day that the three weeks were up, the hen sitting on the hen eggs gave a loud cackle. Belinda rushed up in excitement. "A chick is hatched, a chick is hatched!" she squealed in delight. "Come and see!"

Mike and Ann rushed up. Yes, there was a tiny yellow chick—and then another egg cracked and a second chick came out—and

" Every tiny chick raced to its mother "

then a third and a fourth! The old hen kept
putting her head on one side, and listening
and looking. She was very pleased.

Eleven chicks hatched out of the thirteen
eggs. They were a week old, and running
about all over the place, before the duck eggs
hatched. And oh, what dear little waddly
things the ducklings were! All of them were
yellow, except one black one. Ann couldn't
imagine how they could have been packed

into the eggs because they looked so big
when they uncurled themselves and waddled
about, cheeping.

"There are ten," said Belinda. "Only
ten! I did hope there would be thirteen."

"Well, you have twenty-one new birds,
so you can't grumble," said Ann. "I think
it's marvellous. Oh, aren't the ducklings
lovely! I like them much better than the
chicks."

"What I like is to see the chicks rush to
their mother hen when one of the cats
come near," said Mike. "Look—here's one
of them now. Watch what happens!"

The hen saw the cat and called loudly to
her chicks. "Danger! Come here! Cluck,
cluck, *cluck*!"

And at once every tiny chick raced to its
mother and hid in her fluffed-out feathers.
Not one could be seen.

"There! She's hidden them all," said
Mike. "I say, Belinda—what's the other
hen going to say when her ducklings go into
the pond?"

Ah, what! There's going to be some fun
then!

"THERE'S hardly a day goes by without something happening on a farm," said Mike. "Especially a farm like this that keeps so many animals and birds."

He was right. Day after day something exciting happened. One day the sow had twelve piglets, and it was the greatest fun to go and watch them rush round the enormous old mother sow at top speed, their absurd little tails curled over their backs.

The mother sow was a lazy, fat old thing. "She lies there all day long, and only gets up to eat," said Mike. "Oh, I really *must* get into the sty and tickle some of those piglets. They're so round and pink and comical!"

He climbed over the gate and tried to catch one of the piglets. They were fright-

" I really must *get into the sty "*

ened, and ran about all over the place, squealing.

"Look out, look out!" shouted Belinda suddenly. "The old sow is getting up!"

Sure enough she was. She didn't like to hear her piglets squealing like that. She lumbered up on to her short thick legs—

and then she rushed headlong at Mike! He was so surprised.

She hit him at the back of the knees and he sat down very suddenly indeed. The sow put down her head to bump him, and Mike shot up at once. In a trice he was climbing over the gate, his shorts very muddy and dirty!

Ann and Belinda laughed till they cried.

"Oh, I never thought the old mother pig could move so quickly!" said Ann. "I guess you won't try to catch one of her piglets again, Mike!"

Rascal, Mike's puppy, tried to lick his master's legs clean. He had grown into a bonny little fellow, and followed Mike about like a shadow. Hoppetty played with him a lot, and it was lovely to see the puppy and the lamb frisking round one another.

The twin calves had grown well, too, and no longer had to be fed on milk from the pails. They were out in the fields now, eating what Ann called "grown-up cow food"—hay, turnips, and things like that.

"I wish animals and birds didn't grow up so quickly," complained Ann. "It seems no time at all since Hoppetty was as tiny as a toy lamb—now he almost looks like a sheep, his coat is so thick and woolly."

Auntie Clara at last said firmly that Hoppetty must not run loose any more, but must go and live in the field, or up on the hills with the sheep.

"He's a scamp," she said. "I caught him going up the stairs to look for you this morning, Ann. And *somebody* ate a whole cake that stood cooling in the kitchen. I'm sure it was Hoppetty."

"He won't like living with the sheep," said Ann, with tears in her eyes. "He won't really."

"He'll love it," said Auntie Clara. "But he won't forget you, Ann. He'll always come running when you call him, so don't fret about it."

Auntie Clara was right. Hoppetty liked being with the other growing lambs and the big sheep. He played wonderful games of chase-me, jump-high, and frisk-around with the other lambs, and was always the ringleader when any trouble was about. And he never forgot Ann.

Whenever the little girl came by and called him, Hoppetty came scampering over to her, nuzzling against her, bleating in a little high voice, just as he used to when he was tiny.

"I'm glad you love me still," said Ann, "but oh dear, I do wish you wouldn't grow up into a silly sheep!"

Another excitement was when the ducklings were a few weeks old, and discovered the pond for the first time. All the children were in the yard, having just brought back a big cart-horse from the blacksmith. That was one of their nicest jobs—to take the horses down to the smith to be shod.

They had handed over big Dobbin to their uncle, when he suddenly gave a chuckle and pointed to the pond.

"See there?" he said. "Those new ducklings have seen the pond—now watch old mother hen!"

The hen had no idea at all that her chicks were ducklings. She hated the water. She would not get even a toe wet, and whenever the chicks or ducklings went near the water all the hens nearby set up a warning squawk— "Cluck, cluck, come back, naughty chicks.

Cluck, cluck, don't go near that water!"

And, as soon as the ducklings wandered near that day, their mother hen gave a loud, angry cluck. "Danger! Come back!"

One duckling thought the pond looked fine. He paddled in the water. The hen went nearly mad with fear and rage. She stood at the edge and scolded the daring duckling loudly.

He suddenly went in deeper. He launched his little yellow body on the water like a boat and swam off in the greatest delight, his tiny legs paddling him as if he had done it for years.

Another duckling did the same—and then a third. The mother hen ran up and down, angry and frightened, making a tremendous noise. All the other hens ran up to join in. The children were helpless with laughter, and Uncle Ned let out one of his booming laughs.

Soon all the ducklings were on the pond, bobbing up and down, enjoying themselves with delighted little quacks. What fun they had! "Why, we're ducklings, not chicks!" they told one another. "Think of that!

Soon all the ducklings were on the pond

Aren't we lucky! We'd better tell the old hen that when we get back."

So they did. But she didn't believe them, and rushed them all away from the water at once.

"But that won't be any good, old hen!" called Mike after her. "They'll be in again to-morrow, splashing with joy. You just see!"

They were, of course, and at last the old hen gave them up in despair, and went off to scratch with her friends.

"Something is always happening here," said Mike. "I just *love* Buttercup Farm!"

"CHILDREN, the sheep are to be sheared to-morrow," said Auntie Clara. "Do you want to watch the shearers at work?"

"Oh, of *course*!" said all three at once.

"I've always wanted to see a shearer cut the wool off a sheep," said Mike. "Auntie, is uncle going to have men do it with shears, by hand, or is he going to have a clipping-machine?"

"It's to be done by hand," said his aunt. "It's lucky to-morrow is Saturday, or you wouldn't be able to watch."

"Will Hoppetty be sheared?" asked Ann, looking very solemn. "I don't think I'd like him all shaven and shorn. He wouldn't look like Hoppetty."

"No, he won't be done," said her aunt. "Lambs are allowed to keep their coats for a whole year. Hoppetty will be shorn next year."

"I should think he'll wish he could be done this year," said Belinda. "It's very hot for May, and I'm sure I'd hate to have to wear a woolly coat like Hoppetty in weather like this!"

As soon as they woke up the next day the children heard the sound of baaing and bleating. They looked out of their windows.

"Look! Look! Jamie and Jinny are rounding up the sheep to bring them to the shearing-sheds," said Mike in excitement. "And oh, I do believe Rascal is with them! He's learning to round up the sheep. Oh, isn't he going to be clever!"

"Yes, he'll be a very valuable sheep-dog one day," said Belinda. "You'd be able to sell him for a lot of money!"

"*Oh!* As if I'd ever, ever sell Rascal!" cried Mike, looking so furious that Belinda laughed.

"I didn't mean it," she said. "Not one of us would ever sell Rascal."

The children went out to the shearing-sheds directly after breakfast. There were four men there, all shearers. The children had never seen them before. What a noise of baaing and bleating there was, as the three dogs brought the sheep around the sheds.

One of the shearers caught a sheep, threw it quickly on its side, and tied its legs together, so that it could not struggle and hurt itself on the big shears when its coat was being cut.

Then, as soon as the sheep was quite quiet, the shearer began his work. Clip, clip, clip went his big sharp shears, and to the children's amazement the sheep's thick woolly coat fell off smoothly and cleanly.

"Oh, look—he's peeling the sheep!" said Ann, and the others laughed at her. But it did look as if the sheep were being "peeled", their coats came away so very neatly.

"Good wool, this," said the shearer, looking up at the children. "Fine heavy coats your sheep have got. Ought to fetch a lot of money."

"I'm glad," said Mike. "Uncle Ned wants to buy a new tractor, so he'll be glad of the money. How quick you are, shearer!"

"Well, we've got plenty of work to get through to-day," said the man. "All those sheep to do! We go to another farm on

Monday. Good weather this, for shorn sheep—hot sun, warm wind, mild nights. I've known the poor creatures be shorn just before a bitter-cold spell of weather, and how they must have missed their warm coats then!"

"I expect they're glad to be rid of them now, though," said Belinda watching the gleaming shears snip, snip, snip at the wool. "It's so very hot to-day. Oh—whatever are you doing to that sheep now it's done?"

The shearer had dipped a big brush into a bucket of tar and had daubed something across its shorn back.

"It's a letter B," said Mike. "Oh—B for Buttercup Farm, I suppose."

"That's right," said the man. "Now if they wander, you'll know they're yours. Get along there!"

He had undone the sheep's legs, and sent it out of the shed with a gentle smack. It trotted off, looking very bare and comical.

"I don't suppose they know each other now," said Ann, as sheep after sheep was sheared and sent out into the sun. "I do think they look queer. I am glad that Hoppetty and the other lambs aren't going to be shorn. I'm sure I wouldn't know Hoppetty from the rest if he didn't have his coat on."

Willie the shepherd looked into the shed. "What are the fleeces like?" he asked.

"Good and heavy," said one of the shearers. "Your sheep are healthy, every one of them, shepherd. A fine lot. Best lot of fleeces we've seen this season."

Willie looked pleased. "Oh ay. They're a good lot of sheep," he said. "And we didn't lose a single lamb this year. We've seventeen running in the field."

Hoppetty came sidling into the shed to look for Ann. The shearer caught hold of him. Ann gave a wild cry and flung herself on Hoppetty, pulling him away.

"No, no! That's my pet lamb. He isn't a year old yet. You're not to shear him!"

"It's all right, Missy," said the shearer with a smile, "I was only going to play with him. I could tell he was a pet, the way he looked at us all—in that cheeky way pet lambs always have. He's growing a fine coat already. I'll shear him for you next year."

" I'll shear him for you next year."

"Yes, I'd like that," said Ann. "Will you put an A on him, though, for Ann, because he's mine."

"That I will," said the shearer. "And you tell your uncle to have a nice warm coat made for you out of your lamb's wool. That'll keep you warm all winter!"

"Oh, I *will*," said Ann, her face glowing. "That's a lovely idea! Fancy, Hoppetty, you're wearing your coat this year—but *I* shall be wearing it next year!"

THE summer went by. It was sunny and warm and full of colour. The may spread along the hedges like snow. It faded, and buttercups came to fill the fields with gold.

Then they went and poppies danced by the wayside in bright scarlet petals. They were in among the corn too, and though Ann knew they should not be there she couldn't help thinking how nice the brilliant red was, peeping out of the golden corn.

The corn had been short and green at first. Then it grew taller, and waved about. Then it gradually turned yellow and the ears filled and were heavy.

"You know, I thought Daddy and Mummy would be back by now," said Mike. "They went for six months—and they've been gone for almost seven. It's the summer holidays now. I wish they would come back."

"They've been having a wonderful time together," said Auntie Clara. "They will be very glad to get back to England, though, and to see you again. They *will* be pleased by the look of you—you've grown as fast as the corn, and your faces are as red-brown as the corn in the field!"

"We've had a lovely time here," said Mike. "I loved the hay-making in June. That was fun."

"We shall be here for the reaping of the corn, shan't we?" said Ann anxiously. "I do want to help with that. I want to see a reaper-binder at work, Auntie—what does Uncle call it?—the self-binder. I do want to see that."

"And so you will," said Auntie Clara. "We're going to begin reaping next week. Uncle's borrowing a self-binder from a friend. My word, it's a wonderful machine! It cuts the corn, bundles it into sheaves, and ties each sheaf up before it tosses it back into the field."

"Does it really?" said Ann. "It sounds like magic."

It looked like magic too! All three chil-

" I loved the hay-making "

dren were out early in the cornfield to
watch the self-binder at work. Uncle Ned
sat in the seat of the machine, and it set off
with a great noise. In wonder the children
watched it work.

"Look!" said Belinda. "It goes into the

waving corn—it cuts it—it binds it into
sheaves —ties a bit of string round each
sheaf—and throws them back behind it for
us to pick up and stand into shocks!"

The children watched for a long time. It was wonderful. In front of the machine was the field of waving corn—but behind it was nothing but sheaves in a row!

"Well, well! What about a little work?" said Auntie Clara, coming up. "Look—we must stand these sheaves upright, and make shocks of them. Watch me."

Soon their aunt had made a fine shock, and the children set to work to make shocks of the fallen sheaves too.

"Sixteen sheaves to a shock," sang Mike. "Sixteen sheaves to a shock! I've done twelve shocks. How many sheaves go into twelve shocks!"

"Goodness! Who wants to know a thing like that!" cried Ann. "Oh dear—I can't build my shocks nearly as quickly as you can. Get away, Rascal. You keep knocking my sheaves down!"

"He only wants to help you," said Mike. "Come here, Rascal!"

When Uncle Ned's corn was all cut, and the sheaves were neatly set up in shocks, the fields looked very lovely and peaceful. Each shock had its own shadow, and as the sun went down, the shadows grew longer and longer.

"Thanks for your good work, my dears," said Uncle Ned, coming up. "Now it won't be many days before we cart the corn to the rick-yard—the corn's very dry already."

"Carting the corn to the rick-yard is called harvest home, isn't it?" said Belinda. "Bringing the harvest home. It sounds nice."

The day came when the corn was to be taken to the rick-yard at the farm. Wagons were sent to the field, and Uncle Ned and Jake began to fork the sheaves up into the cart.

"Oh, look!—the wagon's getting very full," shouted Mike. "You've put so many sheaves in, and they're piling higher and higher!"

"We know that!" panted Uncle Ned. "We're having to throw up the sheaves a long way now—it's hard work."

When the cart was full, and no more sheaves could be put into it, Clopper and Davey had to pull it out of the field to the rick-yard.

"Up you get on the top!" shouted Uncle

Ned to Ann and Belinda. "Mike, you can drive Davey and Clopper, can't you? Off you go, then, and we'll begin filling this other wagon."

The heavy wagon moved off, pulled by Davey and Clopper. Mike sat on the front, proud to be taking the harvest home. The two girls sat right on top of the golden sheaves, clutching at them as the wagon swayed down the lane.

"Harvest home!" sang Ann in her little high voice. "Harvest home! We're bringing the harvest home!"

The wagon went slowly into the yard. Belinda saw two people waiting there. She gazed at them, and then gave a great shout of joy.

"Mummy! Daddy! You've come back!"

She and Ann flung themselves down from the wagon, and Mike leapt down from the front. They threw themselves on their father and mother.

"Oh, Mummy, we've had such a wonderful time!" cried Ann. "Have *you*? We've got a puppy and a lamb, and twin calves and heaps of piglets, and . . . "

"And I've got something much better than all those!" said Daddy lifting Ann high above his head so that she squealed like a piglet. "I've got three children again!"

"You've come on the right day," said Mike. "It's harvest home. We've brought the corn home—and you've come home too."

"What a lovely harvest home!" said Mummy, hugging them all. "What a lovely harvest home!"

ENID BLYTON

If you are an eager Beaver reader, perhaps you ought to try some of our exciting Enid Blyton titles. They are available in bookshops or they can be ordered directly from us. Just complete the form below, enclose the right amount of money and the books will be sent to you at home.

☐	THE CHILDREN OF CHERRY-TREE FARM	£1.99
☐	THE CHILDREN OF WILLOW FARM	£1.99
☐	NAUGHTY AMELIA JANE	£1.50
☐	AMELIA JANE AGAIN	£1.50
☐	THE BIRTHDAY KITTEN	£1.50
☐	THE VERY BIG SECRET	£1.50
☐	THE ADVENTUROUS FOUR	£1.50
☐	THE ADVENTUROUS FOUR AGAIN	£1.50
☐	THE NAUGHTIEST GIRL IS A MONITOR	£1.95
☐	THE NAUGHTIEST GIRL IN THE SCHOOL	£1.95
☐	THE ENCHANTED WOOD	£1.99
☐	THE WISHING-CHAIR AGAIN	£1.99
☐	HURRAH FOR THE CIRCUS	£1.75

If you would like to order books, please send this form, and the money due to:
ARROW BOOKS, BOOKSERVICE BY POST, PO BOX 29, DOUGLAS, ISLE OF MAN, BRITISH ISLES. Please enclose a cheque or postal order made out to Arrow Books Ltd for the amount due including 22p per book for postage and packing both for orders within the UK and for overseas orders.

NAME ....

ADDRESS ....

....

Please print clearly.

Whilst every effort is made to keep prices low it is sometimes necessary to increase cover prices at short notice. Arrow Books reserve the right to show new retail prices on covers which may differ from those previously advertised in the text or elsewhere.

HAZEL TOWNSON

If you're an eager Beaver reader, perhaps you ought to try some of our exciting and funny adventures by Hazel Townson. They are available in bookshops or they can be ordered directly from us. Just complete the form below and enclose the right amount of money and the books will be sent to you at home.

☐	THE SPECKLED PANIC	£1.50
☐	THE CHOKING PERIL	£1.25
☐	THE SHRIEKING FACE	£1.50
☐	THE BARLEY SUGAR GHOSTS	£1.50
☐	DANNY—DON'T JUMP!	£1.25
☐	PILKIE'S PROGRESS	£1.95
☐	ONE GREEN BOTTLE	£1.50
☐	GARY WHO?	£1.50
☐	THE GREAT ICE-CREAM CRIME	£1.50
☐	THE SIEGE OF COBB STREET SCHOOL	£1.25

If you would like to order books, please send this form, and the money due to:
ARROW BOOKS, BOOKSERVICE BY POST, PO BOX 29, DOUGLAS, ISLE OF MAN, BRITISH ISLES. Please enclose a cheque or postal order made out to Arrow Books Ltd for the amount due including 22p per book for postage and packing both for orders within the UK and for overseas orders.

NAME . . . .

ADDRESS . . . .

. . . .

Please print clearly.

Whilst every effort is made to keep prices low it is sometimes necessary to increase cover prices at short notice. Arrow Books reserve the right to show new retail prices on covers which may differ from those previously advertised in the text or elsewhere.

BEAVER BOOKS FOR YOUNGER READERS

Have you heard about all the exciting stories available in Beaver? You can buy them in bookstores or they can be ordered directly from us. Just complete the form below and send the right amount of money and the books will be sent to you at home.

☐ THE BIRTHDAY KITTEN	Enid Blyton	£1.50
☐ THE WISHING CHAIR AGAIN	Enid Blyton	£1.99
☐ BEWITCHED BY THE BRAIN SHARPENERS	Philip Curtis	£1.75
☐ SOMETHING NEW FOR A BEAR TO DO	Shirley Isherwood	£1.95
☐ REBECCA'S WORLD	Terry Nation	£1.99
☐ CONRAD	Christine Nostlinger	£1.50
☐ FENELLA FANG	Ritchie Perry	£1.95
☐ MRS PEPPERPOT'S OUTING	Alf Prøysen	£1.99
☐ THE WORST KIDS IN THE WORLD	Barbara Robinson	£1.75
☐ THE MIDNIGHT KITTENS	Dodie Smith	£1.75
☐ ONE GREEN BOTTLE	Hazel Townson	£1.50
☐ THE VANISHING GRAN	Hazel Townson	£1.50
☐ THE GINGERBREAD MAN	Elizabeth Walker	£1.50
☐ BOGWOPPIT	Ursula Moray Williams	£1.95

If you would like to order books, please send this form, and the money due to:
ARROW BOOKS, BOOKSERVICE BY POST, PO BOX 29, DOUGLAS, ISLE OF MAN, BRITISH ISLES. Please enclose a cheque or postal order made out to Arrow Books Ltd for the amount due including 22p per book for postage and packing both for orders within the UK and for overseas orders.

NAME ....

ADDRESS ....

....
Please print clearly.

Whilst every effort is made to keep prices low it is sometimes necessary to increase cover prices at short notice. Arrow Books reserve the right to show new retail prices on covers which may differ from those previously advertised in the text or elsewhere.